Teletubbies™

Tubby Custard Mess

SCHOLASTIC INC.

New York   Toronto   London   Auckland   Sydney

One day in Teletubbyland, it was time for tubby custard.

But then Dipsy had an accident.

Dipsy spilled tubby custard all
over his tubby seat.

Tinky Winky, Laa-Laa and Po sat down on their tubby seats. But Dipsy didn't want to sit down.

Dipsy didn't want to sit in the tubby custard.

Dipsy had nowhere to sit.
So Laa-Laa let Dipsy sit on her tubby seat.

But then Laa-Laa had nowhere to sit.
Laa-Laa didn't want to sit in the tubby custard.

So Po let Laa-Laa sit on her tubby seat.

But then Po had nowhere to sit.
Po didn't want to sit in the tubby custard.

So Tinky Winky let Po sit on his tubby seat.

But then Tinky Winky had nowhere to sit.
Tinky Winky didn't want to sit
in the tubby custard.

Dipsy and Laa-Laa
wanted Tinky Winky
to sit on their tubby
seats.

Tinky Winky couldn't decide which tubby seat to sit on.

Po had an idea. She ran around and sat on another tubby seat.

Tinky Winky sat next to her. But then
Dipsy and Laa-Laa wanted to sit down.

Dipsy and Laa-Laa tried to share a tubby seat.

But there wasn't room!

So Po stood up again.

Dipsy and Laa-Laa tried to share another seat.

But there still wasn't room!

Dipsy sat down on the tubby seat and Laa-Laa had nowhere to sit.

So Laa-Laa sang a song.
Tinky Winky, Dipsy and Po joined in.

While they were
singing, the
Noo-noo tidied up.

Now all the Teletubbies had somewhere to sit. But they were all sitting on the wrong tubby seats!

So the Teletubbies changed places ...

again ... and again ... and again ...

until they were all sitting in the right places.
And then it was time for tubby custard.

Teletubbies love tubby custard.
And Teletubbies love each other very much.

Big hug!

Look for these other Teletubbies storybooks:
Dipsy Dances
Four Happy Teletubbies
Go, Po, Go!

0-590-38616-6

Text adapted from the original scripts by Andrew Davenport.
Text, design, and illustrations copyright BBC Worldwide.
Teletubbies character and logo, copyright and TM 1998 Ragdoll Productions (UK) Ltd.
Licensed by The itsy bitsy Entertainment Company. All rights reserved.
Published by Scholastic Inc.
SCHOLASTIC and associated logos are trademarks
and/or registered trademarks of Scholastic Inc.

12 11 10 9 8 7 6 5 4 3 2 1   8 9/9 0 1 2 3/0

Printed in the U.S.A.

First Scholastic printing, October 1998